D1529897

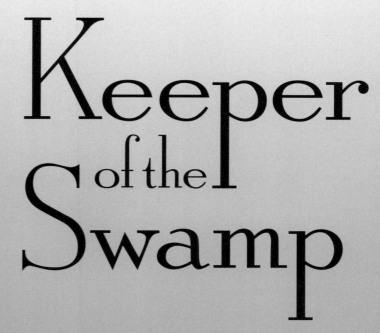

Keeper
of the
Swamp

written by Ann Garrett

illustrated by Karen Chandler

Turtle Books
New York

Sweat trickled down the boy's face. His stomach tightened into a hard knot.

Muddy water lapped against the boat, swaying it gently.

Warm air hung heavy with the sweet scent of flowers. Bullfrogs croaked their songs, dragonflies darted around him.

Today was the day the boy had waited for.

Would he be big enough, would he be strong enough, would he be brave enough?

He gazed up at the old man who pushed the long
pole into the murky water. The old man didn't look sick.
The boy knew better. The old man wouldn't be with him
much longer.

The boat glided deeper into the shadowy swamp,
closer and closer to the 'gator's den. Rags of Spanish
moss hanging from the ancient trees brushed against
the boy's face. Their tattered curtains, speckled with
small delicate flowers, shut out the sun.

A startled heron took flight. The boy jumped at
the sudden flapping. Grandfather had taught the boy
the ways of the swamp. "Don't get too close to any
'gator," he would warn. "A young'un like you is just a
snack."

The boy was the first to see her—the old man's 'gator, Ole Boots. She lay nearby on a muddy bank, so still, that if he hadn't looked closely, he'd have thought she was a log.

All his life, the boy loved to hear the story of the 'gator's rescue—how the old man had found her in the nest just after she'd hatched; just after her mother had been killed by poachers.

"I named her Ole Boots," he'd laugh and say. "Why I saved her hide from being turned into a fancy pair of footwear, Boy. And when she'd grown big enough to hunt, I turned her free in the swamp."

Even now, his grandfather watched over the swamp, running off poachers. "I feel kinship with Ole Boots," he'd say. "That's why she'll do the trick for me. I taught it to her when she was just a 'little one.' Even though she's grown, she's still my 'gator, and I'm her protector."

To the boy, Ole Boots was a wildly fierce creature.

The old man lifted a long wooden rod from the side of the boat. The boy's heart hammered against his chest. Slowly the boy reached for the rod and took a deep breath. "Boy, you don't need to prove anything to me."

From the cooler the boy took a raw chicken breast. Spearing it through with the point of the rod, he threw back his head, and let out the 'gator call: "ka-hah, ka-hah, ka-hah!"

Ole Boots stirred, awakened by the familiar sound. She slipped into the water.

As he'd seen his grandfather do so many times
before, the boy steadied himself, braced the rod on his
hip, and held it out high, over the edge of the boat.

The water parted into a 'V' shape. Two small
eyes riveted on the boy.

The boy could feel the old man's presence as he
stepped closer and stood behind him.

The boy's breath came faster. The 'gator was
right below him. He began to falter, the rod slipping
from his hands.

Ole Boots shot straight up out of the water, razor-sharp teeth glistening.

The boy lurched backwards, falling into his Grandfather's steadying arms. The rod and chicken dropped into the water. The 'gator chomped down on the chicken breast, leaving the rod floating on the surface. Slowly Ole Boots began to circle the boat.

The boy hung his head. "I'm sorry Grandpa."

"That's okay," said the old man. "You tried."

Biting at his trembling lower lip, the boy watched
the circling 'gator.

"Try grasping the rod more firmly, like this," the
old man said. Tenderly, he laid his hand on the boy's
shoulder. The boy nodded.

Cautiously, the boy fished the rod from the hazy water. Again he speared a chicken breast, but this time he held the rod much higher in the air. His muscles tensed as he tightened his grip.

The 'gator spotted the chicken. Her hind legs and tail thrashed deep in the water. She rocketed upward, monstrous jaws spread wide apart, jagged teeth flashing.

Higher and higher Ole Boots rose. Her leathery stomach lunged upward just inches from the boy's face.

He gasped, but didn't let go of the rod.

The 'gator's jaws snapped shut, jerking the rod
and knocking the boy off balance. He stumbled, but
regained his footing.
SPLASH! Ole Boots was gone.

A breath exploded from the boy's lips, "I did it Grandpa! Boots jumped for me!"

Strong arms encircled the boy. He held on tightly to his grandfather. "I'll take good care of Ole Boots for you," he said in a whisper.

The old man gently stroked the boy's hair. "I know you will, Boy. I know you will."

Grandfather pointed toward the sandy bank.
"Look," he said.

The boy didn't understand at first. Then he saw
it—a mound of twigs and leaves near the water's edge.
A gator's nest!

While the boy and the old man watched, Ole Boots lumbered out of the water and returned to her nest. "I've been guarding the eggs," the old man said. "Soon they'll hatch, and we'll have baby alligators."

For the first time that day the old man sat down.
He smiled at the boy. The boy smiled back.

Dusk crept over the swamp.

Bats, awakened from their roosts among the
Spanish moss, skimmed over the water searching for
the insects. Crickets chirped; a raccoon chattered
along the bank, fishing for its dinner.

The boy—the new keeper of the swamp—poled
the boat toward home.

Epilogue

ALLIGATORS

Alligators are reptiles. This means that they are cold-blooded and the same temperature as the water or air around them. Reptiles are the last living relative of the dinosaur. Scientists have found fossils of ancient alligators which were 60 feet long. Today, alligators are much smaller. Males are commonly 9 feet long and weigh about 250 lbs. Females are not as long, nor do they weigh as much. The largest known American Alligator was 19 feet long. They can live to be over 50 years old.

The American Alligator is found in sluggish streams and swamps from North Carolina to Florida and along the Gulf Coast. During the day, alligators spend their time floating just below the surface of the water or resting on muddy banks. They usually hunt by night, both on the banks and in the water. Alligators will lunge out in a flash, clamping their large powerful jaws on their victims. They'll spin and twist in the water to tear off bite-size chunks of meat which they will swallow whole. Alligator teeth are only good for grabbing and tearing; they can't chew their food. This is why alligators swallow stones. These stones help to smash up the food they have eaten and also keep them from bobbing up in the water.

Male alligators make a bellowing roar. This alerts female alligators as to where they are. Female alligators build large nests of plants, rotting leaves, and mud. In this great heap, they dig a hole and lay 15-70 eggs which is called a clutch. The mother then covers the eggs—with more vegetation and mud. Heat from the sun and decaying leaves and plants act as a natural incubator which hatches the eggs in 9-10 weeks. During this time, the mother stands guard to protect her nest from birds and animals which feed on eggs.

When the baby alligators are ready to hatch, they chip away at their shells with tiny teeth. Once hatched, they make a peeping sound which alerts the mother to dig them out of the nest. She then leads her young to the water. These baby alligators live with their mothers until they grow older.

Alligators were once endangered because they were hunted for their skins. There are now laws protecting wild alligators, which have helped their population to grow. American Alligators usually leave people alone, but have been known to attack when threatened. They should be treated with caution and respect as the incredible—but wild and dangerous—creatures they are.

SWAMPS

Swamps, bogs, and marshes are all called wetlands. These wetlands cover seventy million acres of the United States. They provide homes for many plants, animals, and birds which would simply vanish from the Earth without them.

A swamp is an area of land which is immersed by a shallow layer of water. It is dominated by shrubs and trees. The plants and animals which exist in swamps are adapted to living in a watery environment. There are two different types of swamps, saltwater and freshwater.

Keeper of the Swamp takes place in the freshwater swamp of the Louisiana Bayou. "Bayou" is a Native American word meaning creek. The slow-moving, brackish waters of this bayou were once the highways of the Chitimacha, Choctaw, and Chickasaw tribes.

The pirate Jean Lafitte hid in these murky waterways and legend says that pirate gold is buried here.

In this bayou, cypress trees grow to tremendous heights. Spanish moss drapes from their branches, giving the swamp a spooky appearance. More than 500,000 alligators live in Louisiana swamps in addition to cottonmouth snakes, wild boars, beavers, raccoons, and a variety of small animals, birds, and fish. There is even rumor of a swamp monster, a strange creature with orange hair, which stands seven feet tall and weighs 350 pounds!

If ever you are in Louisiana or another large swamp area, there are tours you can join which will take you safely into the swamp. Once there, the swamp may share with you some of its many mysteries.

With deep love and respect
for my Grandmother: "Nanny," Mabel Smith Brandford. (1885-1977) —AG

The author would like to thank the following writers: Gene-Michael Higney, Marion Rosen, Abby Yolles
and Karen Eustis. I will always be grateful. —AG

To my grandfather: "the light of my life"—KC

"American Alligators usually leave people alone, but have been known to attack when
threatened. They should be treated with caution and respect as the incredible—but wild
and dangerous—creatures they are." —Author & Publisher

Keeper of the Swamp

Text copyright © 1999 by Ann Garrett
Illustrations copyright © 1999 by Karen Chandler

First Published in 1999 by Turtle Books

All rights reserved. No part of this book may be used or reproduced in any manner whatsoever
without written permission, except in the case of brief quotations embodied in critical articles and reviews.

Turtle Books is a trademark of Turtle Books, Inc.
For information or permissions, address:
Turtle Books, 866 United Nations Plaza, Suite 525
New York, New York 10017

Cover and book design by Jessica Kirchoff Bowlby
Text of this book is set in Amphora
Illustrations are generated by the use of oil paintings and computer art combined.
First Edition
Printed on 80# White Mountie matte, acid-free paper
Smyth sewn, cambric reinforced binding
Printed and bound in the United States of America

10 9 8 7 6 5 4 3 2 1

Library of Congress Cataloging-in-Publication Data
Garrett, Ann, 1953- Keeper of the swamp / written by Ann Garrett ; illustrated by Karen Chandler. p. cm.
Summary: A boy's heritage from his dying grandfather, who protects the alligators of their Louisiana swamp from
poachers, is the knowledge of the ways of the swamp and how it should be kept undamaged.
Includes informational pages on alligators and swamps.
ISBN 1-890515-12-4 (English hardcover trade edition : alk. paper)
[1. Swamps—Fiction. 2. Alligators—Fiction. 3. Environmental protection—Fiction. 4. Grandfathers—Fiction.
5. Louisiana—Fiction.] I. Chandler, Karen, ill. II. Title.
PZ7.G18447Ke 1999 [E]—dc21 98-40406 CIP AC

Distributed by Publishers Group West

ISBN 1-890515-12-4